ORLANDO RODRIGUEZ

A Ghost Named
FLOSSIE

To order additional copies of this book, contact:
Xlibris
844-714-8691
www.Xlibris.com
Orders@Xlibris.com

ISBN: Softcover 978-1-6641-7781-9
EBook 978-1-6641-7780-2

Library of Congress Control Number: 2021911026

Print information available on the last page

Rev. date: 07/24/2021

A GHOST NAMED FLOSSIE

To my father, who was a loving and caring father, and to my mother, who is the best mother in the world. Dad, I miss you and wish you were still here. Mom, I thank God that you are still here with me. I don't know where I would be without the both of you.

Chapter 1

A Strange Customer

Dickinson was a city in Texas fifteen minutes away from Houston. It was a welcoming town, and many people had lived there for years. Right in the middle of Dickinson was a friendly gas station called the Filler Upper. Many people went to this gas station not just for gas but also for the hospitality that they received there. The workers were genuinely nice to their customers; many times, customers got free soda.

One of the customers' favorite cashiers was Seth Ramirez. Seth was a nineteen-year-old who had been working at the Filler Upper since he was sixteen. He started out as a stocker and was now a cashier while attending college in Texas City. Seth was a happy young man, but something was going to happen to him that would change his life forever.

It was a gloomy day in Dickinson. The clouds looked ominous, and the wind was strong. It was five o'clock in the morning, and Seth had just arrived. Seth worked in the morning and went to college at night. While he was getting everything ready for the day, he had a bad feeling that he could not explain. Something did not seem quite right. As he was organizing the front area, he noticed a young lady outside who looked dazed and lost. She walked right to the window and then stopped and stared into the store. Seth was kind of frightened by her behavior and her mysterious look, yet he stayed calm. He smiled at this strange-looking girl and told her that the gas station was closed. Seth hoped she could hear him through the window. He waited for a response. She stayed in that same position and did not talk or move. She did not even blink. Again, Seth told her that the gas station was not open. Still the same response from this mysterious girl. Seth gave up and walked away. When he turned the corner, he looked back, and she was gone. How could this be? She was just there, and then she was gone! It was as if she'd disappeared! Seth quickly walked out of the store to see whether she was around the side of the store, but she was not. There was no other place that she could be because the back gate was locked. Seth got knots in his stomach, and that strange feeling he had earlier became more vigorous. Now he had an idea why he felt the way he felt. But what he did not realize was that the girl was a ghost.

Chapter 2

A Ghost In The Store

It was now six in the morning, and it was time to open. As Seth unlocked the door and turned on the open sign, he looked around to see if the mysterious girl was around. He walked outside again to see if she was around the corner so that he could let her in, but he did not find her. Then he went back in, and there she was, standing in front of the counter. Seth was shocked and could not believe his eyes. She was nowhere to be found, and then all of a sudden she was in the store. *How did she get past me?* he thought. Seth quickly walked around the girl to the front of the counter and asked her how he could help her. She stood there very mysteriously. Seth could not help but notice a strange looking white dress, and her hair covering her face. Her shoes looked more like slippers. Seth did not know what to do. He could not get this girl to talk, and he had duties to perform. He did not want to be rude and leave her standing there, so he asked her again if she needed any help.

At last she said, "Can you give me a ride to my house?"

He gave her an odd look. “No, ma’am. I am working and cannot leave.”

She stood still and stared at him. She did not speak again, so Seth asked if he could call her a cab. She did not answer. She turned away very slowly, walked out of the gas station, and sat on the bench outside by the door. Seth continued his work, wondering what was going on. He could not believe that he was going through this. Nothing like this had ever happened to him before. During the day, he could not stop thinking about her. He wondered who she was and where she was from.

Chapter 3

A Visit to the Woods

It was three o'clock, and Seth's shift was over. He clocked out and left as he usually did, but he still felt uncomfortable about what had happened earlier. The girl was gone, and the bench was empty. Seth was kind of relieved because he did not want anything to do with that strange girl. Seth started home. As he drove off, he noticed a girl walking on the side of the road. His eyes almost popped out of his face. It was that same girl! Seth could not believe it. He did not want to stop to help her, but he did not want to ignore her either. He hesitated and then pulled over, rolled his window down, and asked her if she wanted a ride. She did not answer, but she opened the door and got in the car. He asked her where she lived. She did not answer and kept looking forward. He asked again, and still no response. He told her that he needed to know where to take her. She stayed silent. Seth told her that if she did not tell him where she lived, she would have to get out of his car. She still said nothing and just sat there, looking as mysterious as ever. Seth did not want to kick her out of his car, and he knew it was not safe to stay on the side of the road, so he decided to take her to the police station. Seth started driving and could not wait to get to the police station.

On the way to the police station, the mysterious girl said, “Pull over,” so he did. Seth was shocked but did what she said. As he looked around, he noticed there were no houses or stores, just woods. She got out of the car and walked toward the woods. Seth got out of the car and told her not to go into the woods. He promised her that he would take her to her house, but she did not listen and kept walking. He wanted to follow her but felt that it was too risky because he did not know who she was or what she was about. The girl kept walking until Seth could not see her. He got into his car and left. All the way home, he wondered who she was, why she would not say where she lived, and why she went into the woods. Seth went home feeling extremely uncomfortable.

The next day, Seth was back at work as usual. He hoped that this strange girl would not return. During his lunch hour, he decided to eat behind the store. As he sat down, he felt someone staring at him. He looked up, and there she was—that same mysterious girl was staring at Seth. Being the nice person that he was, Seth called her over. As she approached him, he asked if she was OK.

At first she did not respond, but then she said, “Can you give me a ride to my house?”

He gave her a very odd look and said, “I tried, but you told me to pull over, and then you got out of the car and walked into the woods.”

She said nothing. It was quiet for about ten seconds, and she asked again, "Can you give me a ride to my house?"

Seth was really confused. He felt like he was talking to a deaf person. Again Seth stated that he had tried but was not successful. "In order for me to take you home, I need to know where you live."

When she didn't reply, Seth gave up and started eating his lunch. He offered her some of his lunch, but she did not answer—something Seth was getting accustomed to. Both were quiet.

After five minutes she said, "I am lost."

Seth replied, "Why didn't you say that earlier? What is your name?"

She said, "Flossie."

"Great," Seth said. "Now we are getting somewhere. Flossie what?"

She just repeated herself. "Flossie."

Seth knew that he was not going to get any more information out of her, so he left it alone. He finished his lunch very quickly and told her that he had to go but would be able to take her to her house when he got off work.

HALLOWEEN

It was three o'clock again, and Seth had finally finished his shift. As he walked to his car, he looked around for Flossie. He did not see her in the front of the store, so he drove to the back. She was not there, so he headed home. On his way home, he saw Flossie walking in the opposite direction. He quickly turned around so he could give her a ride, but when he drove up behind her, she turned toward the woods. It was déjà vu. He called out her name, but she kept walking toward the woods until he could not see here anymore. He wondered what was in the woods that she found so interesting. He wondered why she kept going into the woods; it puzzled him. All the way home, he kept thinking about Flossie and the woods. Later, he decided to give it up.

Seth did not think about her or see her for weeks. He really thought it was over—until Halloween night.

It was just past midnight in the early hours of Halloween, and Seth was driving home from a friend's house. He saw a young girl walking on the side of the road. He felt sorry for her and wanted to help her. He knew it was dangerous for a young girl to be walking on the side of road this late. He pulled over to ask her if she needed any help. As he got closer to her, he realized that the girl was Flossie. He had thought he would never see her again. *This is going to be a weird Halloween,* he thought.

He asked her if she needed a ride, and she said yes. She got in the car and said, "Can you give me a ride to my house?" He asked where, and she did not answer. He was not going to go through this again. He told her that he was getting upset with her because he felt like she was playing games. He asked her again, but this time he said it firmly. Seth was tired of Flossie not telling him where she lived. Still, she did not answer and stayed as still as a statue.

Seth had a plan. He thought if she were to pull the same stunt again, asking him to stop at the side of the road so she could go into the woods, he would not stop this time. So off they went. Soon she said, "Pull over." It was the same spot she had said last time, but Seth kept going. She repeated herself, and Seth did not comply. All of a sudden, the car pulled itself over. Seth felt someone turn the steering wheel with a strength that he could not control. But who was it? No one was in the car except him and Flossie, and her hands never touched the steering wheel. The next thing Seth knew, he was on the side of the road, and Flossie was getting out of the car. It happened so fast that Seth did not have time to figure out why the car pulled itself over. He simply wanted to follow Flossie.

Flossie got out of the car and did the same thing she always did: walk straight to the woods. This time, Seth followed her right into the woods. He waited before he started to follow her because he did not want her to hear him following. As he started walking, he knew he had to hurry up because he did not want to lose her, especially in the dark on Halloween. He started walking faster, but by the time he entered the woods, she had disappeared. He was shocked. She had disappeared practically right before his eyes! He had his flashlight, but that did not help. How could she have disappeared so fast? *Only witches are able to do that,* he thought. He looked around but still could not see her. Being in the woods on Halloween was a freaky feeling, so he left. He still could not believe what had just happened and was bewildered about the situation.

Then Seth had a strange thought. Wouldn't a young girl be scared to go into the woods in the middle of the night. especially on Halloween? Wasn't she scared someone might attack her? "Maybe she's a ghost. I just know I saw her disappear right before my eyes. She probably is a *fantasma*." That was *ghost* in Spanish. He giggled and thought, *There is no such thing as ghosts. It's dark. Maybe it just looked like she disappeared. He went back to his car and continued to worry about Flossie.* "Maybe a wild animal ate her," he said to himself. "Or maybe a man was already in the woods and kidnapped her." Seth was going crazy wondering what had happened to Flossie.

As he arrived home, he noticed something weird while still in his driveway. He looked up toward his bedroom window and saw the curtains slowly pull apart, as if someone was in his room looking out the window. He went in the house and went straight to his room, and the curtains were closed. To make things even more strange, nobody was home. Seth could not understand how his curtains were open from the outside but closed from the inside. He knew he had seen them open. The house was empty. Who could have done this? Seth's parents had gone out for the evening and were not back yet. The fact that it was Halloween could not have something to do with the curtains opening. Or could it?

Seth realized that ever since he had met Flossie, weird things had been happening. One time during his shift, the lights kept going on and off, and that had never happened before. He sat down and thought about it. *This girl just shows up out of nowhere. She always has a mysterious look on her face, and she never tells me exactly where she lives, but she keeps asking for a ride home. And the weirdest thing of all, she keeps going to the woods.* Seth had to sit down and absorb all of this. Finally, he decided that he was going to tell his mother. He went to bed but could not get his mind off Flossie.

31 october

Chapter 5

Halloween Night

It was six in the morning, still on Halloween, and Seth was opening up for the day. He was keeping his eye out for Flossie. It was soon noon, and no Flossie. Seth's boss was named Charlie Rodriguez. Seth had always looked up to his boss, and he had always been on good terms with him. He wanted to tell his boss about Flossie, but he hesitated. He decided to do it some other time.

At three o'clock, Seth headed home. While driving, Seth was kind of nervous because he felt like he would see Flossie. He made it all the way home, and no Flossie.

Seth went straight home and told his mother everything. His mother thought he was making everything up. She told him to stop playing around and get serious. Seth decided to leave it alone, and he walked away. Seth's mom was preparing for the trick-or-treaters. As Seth was walking up the stairs, the phone rang. It was his boss, Charlie. He wanted to know if Seth was able to work this Halloween night. The other cashier wanted to take his child trick-or-treating, so he needed the night off. Charlie wanted to know if Seth could take his place. Seth said yes.

What would happen at his job during this Halloween night would scare Seth almost half to death. Had Seth known what was going to happen, he would have said no.

Seth made it to work and thought that this would be a good time to tell Charlie about Flossie. Before Charlie left work, Seth asked him if he could stay for a few minutes so he could talk to him. Charlie, who was like a father to Seth, said he would not mind. Seth sat him down and told him everything about Flossie. Charlie giggled and said, "Is this a Halloween story?"

"No," said Seth. "This is really true."

Charlie indicated that the story sounded odd and laughed. Like Seth's mother, he did not take Seth seriously.

Seth let it go and went on with his business. He could not believe that no one took him seriously. *How can I get people to believe me?* As Seth thought about it, he hoped he would never see Flossie again. Seth hoped that the night would not go by slowly and that it would be filled with trick-or-treaters. However, at eight o'clock, no customers were coming in, not even the trick-or-treaters. Seth was sitting there and wondering why the night was dragging. *It's Halloween. Where are the trick-or-treaters?* he thought.

All of a sudden, the lights turned off. Seth yelled, "Who is here? Who turned off the lights?" No answer. Seth walked to the light switches, and they all were on. *Oh, no,*

Seth thought. *Flossie.* He did not know what to do. He looked around but saw no one. The lights came back on, and Seth stood still, scared. Now he heard a noise in the back like something had fallen. He was scared to go back and look, but he knew he had to. He walked very slowly because if there was someone back there, he did not want them to hear him walking in their direction. He opened the door slowly and saw no one. He was relieved but still confused as to where the noise had come from. When he went back to the front, he noticed the newspapers on the floor. They were not on the floor before he left. How did they get on the floor? He was the only one in the store. Again he thought, *Flossie.*

The lights turned back off, and he heard a girl's voice say, "Help me." Seth froze. Again he heard the voice say, "Help me." He immediately got on the phone and tried calling his mother, but the phone was dead. Seth was really scared. It was Halloween, and weird things were happening.

Finally, everything went back to normal. Seth sat there worried because he did not want to know what was going to happen next. It was now 10:00 p.m., and Seth clocked out. He had to hurry home because he had to open the store at 6:00 a.m. He also wanted to get out of the gas station after what had happened. He hoped he would not see Flossie, and if he did, he was not going to stop. Luckily for him, he did not see her. Seth arrived home safely, got ready for bed, and tried to forget about all that happened. He did not even want to tell his mother what had happened. All he wanted to do was get on with his life and not think about Flossie. But Flossie was not going to let that happen.

The next morning, it was a new day for Seth. He got out of bed and started his day as usual. When he got to work, he checked the phone, and miraculously it was working. He wanted to rewind the cameras so he could prove that there was a girl named Flossie, but the cameras were frozen and had been for a long while. As a matter of fact, they had been frozen ever since Flossie had first arrived. He could not believe this. Now no one would believe him. *Did Flossie do this?* He thought. He did not want to ponder on it and kept working.

Two weeks went by, and no Flossie. Seth knew for sure he was never going to see her again. Even though his gut feeling told him different, he still managed to believe the opposite.

Chapter 6

An Unpleasant Visit

Seth was on his way to school. The day was gloomy, and Seth did not catch on. Catch on to the fact that it was a gloomy day when he had first met Flossie. Seth was not thinking of Flossie. As the night continued, Seth worked diligently. By the time Seth left school, it was dark outside. He walked to his car, put his books in the trunk, and got in his car. As Seth started the car, he heard a voice say, "Can you give me a ride to my house?" He almost jumped out of the window. Then he turned around, and there she was. Flossie sitting in his back seat.

Seth couldn't help himself and yelled, "What are you doing in my car, and how did you get in?"

She simply said, "Help me." Those were the same words he had heard on Halloween night.

"So that was you," he said. "What do you want from me? Why are you doing this to me?"

Flossie simply sat there and repeated, "Help me."

Seth said, "I do not know how to help you. Please get out of my car." Flossie remained still.

Seth had no choice but to get out, walk to the campus police, and report what had just happened. When Seth and the cops walked back to his car, Flossie was gone. The cops did not know what to think of this situation. Seth apologized and said, "I hope the both of you don't think I am lying."

"No, I believe you," the officer said.

Seth got back in the car and was frightened the whole way home. *How does Flossie want me to help her?* he thought. *Why won't she leave me alone?* The more he thought about it, the more it frightened him. He decided to talk to his friend Edgar.

Edgar Orozco was known to speak to the dead. He had been doing this for more than twenty-five years. Seth knew that Edgar would be the one to talk to about this. He was going to call the next morning while he was at work. On his way home, Seth felt very uneasy and kept looking in his rearview mirror to make sure Flossie was not in the back seat. He finally made it home and went straight to bed. He hoped he would fall asleep quickly so that he would not have to hear any strange noises. He also did not want to think about this strange, mysterious girl. The night went by, and Flossie was nowhere to be found.

Seth woke up and got ready for work. The first thing that Seth thought about was Flossie. He was glad he hadn't heard from her. Seth was soon at work and performing his normal duties. He waited for nine o'clock so he could call Edgar. Seth briefly explained what was going on. Also, he let Edgar know that he was scared. Edgar told Seth that he had nothing to worry about and this was not unusual. Many people go through this; it's just not talked about. Edgar told Seth to meet him in his office this coming Friday so he could talk more about it. Seth said OK and hung up. Seth could not wait until then because he really wanted to find out what Flossie was all about.

Chapter 7

Flossie and her games

It was now three, and Seth was clocking out to go home. From where he was clocking out, he could see out of the window, and he saw Flossie. He was shocked and could not move. He felt something holding him from making any kind of movement. His boss noticed his odd actions and asked if he was OK. He told his boss that the girl he had told him about was outside. When Charlie looked out the window, she was gone. Charlie did not see anyone, and this made Seth worried. She had just been there. How did she disappear so fast? Now Seth believed she was a ghost.

All of a sudden, Seth was able to move. It was weird, as if something had let him go. He and Charlie looked for Flossie but could not find her. Seth's boss laughed and thought that Seth was back to his crazy stories again. Seth told his boss that his story was not made up—he really had seen Flossie outside. "Sure," Charlie said. His boss went back inside, leaving Seth a little embarrassed.

What could she want? Seth thought. Why is she back? Seth got another freaky feeling. At this time, he wanted nothing to do with Flossie. Seth was on his way home, but this time he decided to take another way home because he did not want to see her again. He was almost home and was at the last red light before he reached his house. As he stopped, he noticed a young girl standing on the corner. Sure enough, it was Flossie. He could not believe his eyes. He ignored her and headed home. Seth was tired of Flossie and did not want to deal with her again. As he rolled into his driveway, he noticed the open curtains in his room again. He did not want to go through this again. He stayed in his car and was afraid to get out. He did not want to look at his window for fear that he might see Flossie.

Seth headed toward his backyard and started playing with his dog, Grunt. Grunt was a dalmatian. As a kid, Seth's favorite book had been *101 Dalmatians*. He had always wanted one, and two years ago he had finally bought a dalmatian from the pet shop. Grunt was playful and very protective, always watching out for Seth and his family. After Seth was finished playing with Grunt, he washed up and started eating his dinner. His mom had made his favorite dish, burrito casserole. Seth had loved eating burritos while growing up, and one day his mom had decided to make him a burrito casserole. It had been his favorite dish ever since. It had tortilla at the bottom with a layer of beans, a layer of ground beef, and a layer of Spanish rice. Mexican cheese topped the casserole, along with onions and red sauce. It was delicious and now a regular dish in the Ramirez household.

The Ramirez family had always been on the right side of the law. Mr. Ramirez was a cop, and Mrs. Ramirez was a teacher. Seth was an only child and loved life just as much as he loved his parents. Seth loved helping people, just like his parents. He was in college studying social work, and he couldn't wait to start working. The gas station was just a job to help support him through college; he wouldn't be there for long. In the meantime, Seth made the best of everything. He loved his job, his boss, and his colleagues. Seth had always been an obedient child and could get along with others. He was the type of person who will help anyone. That was one reason he was always trying to help Flossie, despite her mysteriousness.

Dinner was soon over, and Seth cleaned up and went to bed.

The Meeting with the Medium

Friday morning came, but not soon enough for Seth. The moment he had been waiting for has arrived. He and Edgar sat down and started talking about Seth's situation. After Seth was done, Edgar said that he knew what was going on. He told Seth that Flossie was a ghost. It startled Seth, and he could not believe his ears. Even though he had that suspicion, he still could not believe what Edgar was telling him. "I knew I saw her disappear the other day," said Seth. "Go on."

"Well," continued Edgar, "it seems that Flossie has some unfinished business, and you are the only one who can help her."

"How can I help her?" asked Seth. "I don't know what to do."

"She is trying to tell you. You say she keeps going to the woods, right? Well, Flossie is trying to take you there because something may have happened there, or something is there that she wants to show you. I can't tell you what is in the woods, but I can tell you that you might find your answer there. You see, ghosts can talk like we can, but they can say only so much. Flossie's speech is limited, and therefore, you will have to go to the woods and find out what she is trying to show you."

Seth explained that he had gone in the woods once and had not seen anything, so he'd left.

"How long were you there?" Edgar asked.

Seth replied, "About five minutes."

"You were not there long enough, and you did not know you were supposed to be looking for something." Edgar then told Seth something that Seth did not want to hear. "If you want to get rid of Flossie, you have to go into the woods and stay there to see if she has something to say or something to show you."

"When do I go to the woods?" Seth asked.

"You will have to wait for her to come back. This time when she goes into the woods, you follow her and stay there until you figure out what is going on. I have a strong feeling that you will find your answer."

"In the woods," Seth replied.

"Yes," Edgar said. "Your answer is in the woods. Also, please note that not all ghosts are mean."

"Do you think she wants to hurt me?" asked Seth.

"No," said the spiritual medium. "I feel that she wants to tell you something important. Maybe not important to you, but important to her. Like I said earlier, I feel that she has some unfinished business. She was going to do something, but she died before she could do it."

Seth sat there feeling uncomfortable.

"Well, you won't find out until you follow her into the woods," Edgar said.

As Seth left he continued to feel uncomfortable, but there was nothing he could do. The last thing he wanted to do was follow a ghost into the woods.

Chapter 9

Flossie Is Back

It had been a couple of days, and Seth had not seen Flossie. *Maybe she got someone else to help her,* Seth thought. He hoped that this was true, but still he had a weird feeling that she would return soon.

It was soon 10:00 p.m., and Seth was in bed. He was still thinking of Flossie and had not said a thing to anyone. If they had not believed him in the beginning about a strange girl, then for sure they would not believe him if he said she was a ghost. As Seth was laying in bed, he heard Grunt barking. *Grunt never barks in the night.* He looked out of his window into the side yard and saw Flossie standing there, looking at up at Seth. *Oh, no, she's back. What do I do?*

He stepped back, hoping that when he looked again, she would be gone. But the dog kept barking. He knew that Grunt was able to see a ghost from what Edgar had said. He said children and animals were able to see ghosts more often than adults. Seth knew he had to do something. He had to build the courage, go out there, and let Flossie know that he was ready for his mission. He did just that. Seth didn't know whether he should meet her on the side of the house or simply get in his car, knowing that she would probably appear. He decided to go to his car and sit. Sure enough, Flossie appeared right before his eyes. She remained the same Flossie as usual, but this time she said, "Going my way?" Seth said yes. He knew exactly where she wanted to go.

As he got closer to the woods, he expected Flossie to tell him to pull over, and she did. Seth pulled over, and she got of the car and headed toward the woods Seth got out with his flashlight and started to follow. He thought, *Why couldn't she do this in the daytime. Why did she have to pick the night?* As Seth walked, he kept his eyes on Flossie to see if she was going to disappear. Finally, they reached the woods, and Flossie walked to a spot by a big, old rock. She kneeled down and started crying with her head on the rock. Seth hoped she would start talking to give him some kind of information as to what he needed to do, but she kept crying. He asked her how he could help her, but she didn't respond. Seth looked around to see if he could see anything. Being in the woods at night with a ghost was not his idea of entertainment, but Seth knew he had to finish this task. Seth moved his flashlight all over the woods, hoping he would not see a bear or a snake.

Just then, Flossie slowly started to disappear. Seth stared in amazement. He told her, "Stop! Don't go, Flossie! Please tell me what you want from me!" But Flossie kept fading away. "Wait, Flossie! Wait! I'll do whatever you want—just talk to me, please! Don't leave me, Flossie." Still she kept fading away, very slowly.

When she finished disappearing, he noticed a card on the ground where Flossie was at. He picked it up, and it said, "To Mom, from Flossie." On the other side was an address. Seth knew exactly where the address was. He left and decided to go to that address in the morning.

Chapter 10

Seth Finds Flossie's House

It was now morning, and Seth got out of bed. He jumped in the shower and thought about the night before. He was kind of nervous about going to this address because he did not know what to expect. As he got in the car, he felt eerie. Nevertheless, Seth was on his way. He knew he had to finish his mission.

As he arrived, his heart beat fast. He did not want to get out of his car . He opened the car door and slowly walked to the house. When he reached the door, he turned to his left and saw a woman looking at him from the window. He knocked on the door, and she walked over and opened it. "Can I help you?" she asked. Seth looked at her, and then he noticed a picture behind her hanging on the wall. It was Flossie. He could not believe it. It was the ghost that kept following him around!

He looked at the woman and said, "I was hunting in the woods, and I found this card. I think it belongs to you." Seth did not want to tell her what really happen, so he decided to fib. He then handed her the card.

She took it and said, “Flossie! It’s from my daughter.” She started crying. “Where did you say you found this?”

“In the woods,” Seth said.

She said, “Not the woods on Highway 646, by the railroad tracks?”

“Yes,” Seth said frantically. “Why?”

“Because my daughter was killed three years ago. Her body was found in the woods in that same area. She was going to the store to buy me a birthday card, but she was killed before she could make it home.”

“I’m sorry to hear that, ma’am,” Seth said.

“She had a flat tire on her way home. When she never came home, I went to look for her and saw her car with a flat tire on the side of the road. I drove to the nearest store and called the cops. It was then that they found her in the woods, dead. It was the worst day of my life. Witnesses say that they saw her walking on the side of the road. I’m assuming she was walking to the nearest store to call for help. The man who committed this awful crime was caught, and later confessed. He said that he saw my daughter walking away from her car. He noticed she had a flat tire and pretended that was going to help her. He then dragged her into the woods and committed the crime. A witness came forward and told the cops what he saw, giving a description of the man. Still, when I drove the car home, there was nothing in the car. When she was picked up from the woods, no one saw the card, but they did find her purse. That's what puzzles me. Why didn't they see the card if it was in the woods? You saw it."

Seth did not know what to say.

"This card looks fresh. It does not look like it's been in the woods for three years," said the woman.

Seth looked at the card once more and thought the same thing. "How can a card made of paper be in the woods for three years and not be wet or worn out?" That was unbelievable. Then Seth thought, *Maybe Flossie took it with her to her grave, and she brought it back.* He did not want to say anything to her mother.

Flossie's mother asked, "How did you know where to bring the card?"

Seth answered, "The address is on the back of the card."

She turned the card around and said, "There is no address on this card."

Seth took the card and looked, and to his surprise the address was gone. "How could this be?" he said. "I just saw the address on the card. How else would I have known how to get here?"

They looked at each other and both said, "Flossie."

Flossie's mom said, "I bet my daughter put it on there for you to see." Seth agreed. She asked Seth if he wanted to come inside, and Seth accepted. As they sat in the living room, Seth could not help but wonder what the card said. He did not want to ask her to open it because that would be rude—it was none of his business. Also, he did not want to make her cry.

Flossie's mother apologized to Seth and said her name was Mary. Mary asked Seth if he had any sisters, hoping to compare his sisters to Flossie. "No," replied Seth. "I am an only child."

Mary smiled and said, "So was Flossie." She then opened the card. Tears rolled down her cheeks as she read the card silently, but she was smiling the whole time. She then read the card out loud. She wanted Seth to know simply because he had gone out of his way to bring the card; if it were not for Seth, she would not have had the birthday card in her hands.

"Happy birthday, Mom. You are the best mother in the whole wide world, and I love you. Thank you for being a wonderful mother. Love, Flossie."

Seth got out of his seat, gave Mary a hug, and said, "I bet Flossie was a lovely child."

"Oh, yes, she was," said Mary.

Seth decided to leave so she could be alone. As he walked out the door, Mary said, "Don't be a stranger. You are always welcome in my house." Seth smiled and walked away.

Seth would never know why Flossie picked him, but nevertheless, he was glad she did. It made him feel happy inside knowing that he helped someone, even if it was a ghost. Seth could be sure now he would never see Flossie again. The mission was complete. All she wanted was to make sure her mother got her birthday card. As long as Seth lives, he will never forget that he met a ghost named Flossie.

absorbed: took in (knowledge, attitudes, etc.)

bewildered: deeply or utterly confused or perplexed

bizarre: strikingly out of the ordinary; odd, extravagant, or eccentric in style or mode

comply: to conform, submit, or adapt (as to a regulation or to another's wishes) as required or requested

déjà vu: a feeling that one has seen or heard something before

demeanor: behavior toward others; one's outward manner

diligently: characterized by steady, earnest, and energetic effort

eerie: so mysterious, strange, or unexpected as to send a chill up the spine

fabricate: to make up for the purpose of deception

fantasma: ghost in Spanish

fib: a trivial or childish lie

firmly: in a firm manner

frantically: in a nervously hurried, desperate, or panic-stricken way

gen·u·ine·ly- to the fullest degree; properly.

hospitality: hospitable treatment, reception, or disposition

obedient: submissive to the restraint or command of authority; willing to obey

ominous: being or exhibiting an omen

ponder: think about; reflect on

puzzled: to be uncertain as to action or choice

vigorous: carried out forcefully and energetically